Bumble Rumble

Bumble Rumble

Lucy Mayflower

Hodder
Children's
Books

A division of Hodder Headline Limited

Special thanks to Lucy Courtenay

Created by Hodder Children's Books and Lucy Courtenay
Text and illustrations copyright © 2006 Hodder Children's Books
Illustrations created by Artful Doodlers

First published in Great Britain in 2006
by Hodder Children's Books

1

A Catalogue record for this book is available from the British Library

ISBN – 10: 0 340 91180 8
ISBN – 13: 978 0 340 91180 8

Printed and bound in Great Britain
by Bookmarque Ltd, Croydon, Surrey

The paper and board used in this paperback by Hodder Children's Books
are natural recyclable products made from wood grown in
sustainable forests. The manufacturing processes conform to the
environmental regulations of the country of origin.

Hodder Children's Books
A division of Hodder Headline Limited
338 Euston Rd, London NW1 3BH

Contents

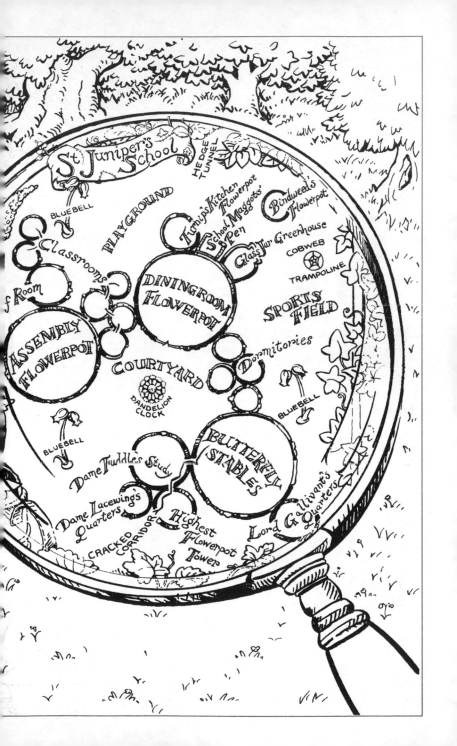

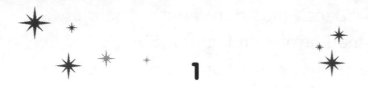

1

A Very Hot Hedgehog

Down at the bottom of the garden, the leaves were beginning to fall. Six fairies huddled together in a clearing, toasting berries on a flickering twig bonfire.

"Last year, Jasmine was almost knocked out by a sycamore seed," said a dark-haired fairy. She peered anxiously up at the trees that loomed overhead, and cuddled the glossy black ant on her lap.

"This is a beech tree, Sesame," said the blonde fairy next to her. One of her earring spiders gave a tiny sneeze, and she reached up and stroked it. "The worst that can happen is a bit of beech nut."

"Beech nuts hurt, Nettle," said a small fairy with feeling. She pulled her berry out of the bonfire and prodded it hopefully. "Kelpie threw one at me once."

"I did not!" shot back a grumpy-looking fairy in a long black and yellow scarf, who was lying on her back with her head resting on a very furry bumblebee. "You just got in the way, Tiptoe."

"In the way of what?" Tiptoe demanded, putting her berry back in the fire.

Kelpie grinned. "Dame Taffeta."

"I flew on a sycamore seed once," boasted the spiky-haired fairy nearest the fire. "I spun round and round on it until I was sick. We all do it in China."

"You've never been to China, Ping," said the prettiest fairy, taking a bite out of her steaming hot berry.

Ping clicked her tongue in annoyance.

"You're such a spoilsport, Brilliance."

The bonfire flickered and spat. The flames were creeping up the pile of twigs, licking towards the sky.

"The Humans at the House will see us," Sesame began, looking concerned as the flames jumped and wavered in the misty air. The ant pushed at her hand for more cuddling.

"I don't care," said Brilliance. "We can fly away, can't we? Anyway, no one ever believes Humans when they say they've seen fairies. Pass me another berry, Tiptoe."

The bonfire crackled and grumbled.

"Is it my imagination," said Nettle cautiously, "or did the bonfire just move?"

The fairies stared at the fire.

"There!" Sesame squeaked. "That twig shivered!"

"I don't like this," Tiptoe said, moving backwards very fast.

The pile of burning twigs shook and fell away, revealing a very large, very cross, very hot-looking hedgehog.

"I thought that you checked the twigs before you lit them, Brilliance!" Ping said.

"I never check anything," said Brilliance loftily.

The hedgehog growled. The fairies stared up into its furious bead-black eyes. Some of its prickles were smouldering. Kelpie's bumblebee Flea shot into the air, buzzing nervously.

"Why aren't we running away?" Tiptoe whispered, staring at the hedgehog.

"Speak for yourself!" Kelpie said, scrambling to her feet and dashing for the Hedge.

Yelling and tumbling, the other fairies followed as the hedgehog gave chase. Sesame held her ant tightly under one arm as they pushed through a narrow bramble patch in the Hedge.

"I tore my wing!" Sesame groaned, looking over her shoulder in dismay. The ant chattered sympathetically at her.

"Better than being pronged by the hedgehog," said Kelpie.

Puffing and panting, the fairies

collapsed among the brambles. They peered through the tall, twisting stems at the angry face of the hedgehog. Ping stuck out her tongue and made a rude noise. The hedgehog blinked at them, then lumbered out of sight.

"Brilliant," said Brilliance with satisfaction.

"I don't see what's so brilliant about it," said Sesame gloomily, examining the tear in her wing. "I'll have to mend this tonight. You should have checked the bonfire, Brilliance. Everyone knows that the hedgehogs are starting to hibernate now."

Nettle looked alert. "Shh!" she hissed. "I can hear something."

They all turned and stared into the depths of the Hedge. High fairy voices could be heard, approaching through the undergrowth. The Naughty Fairies snuggled down and stayed very quiet.

"I'm thure that inkcap muthroomth

grow here," squeaked the tiniest voice. "Lady Campion thayth . . ."

"You shouldn't believe everything Lady Campion says, Glee," drawled another voice. "She may be our head teacher, but Mummy says she's common."

"Ambrosia Academy fairies!" breathed Tiptoe with wide eyes. Ambrosia Academy was a school for rich fairies in the nearby Wood.

Three fairies came into view, flying daintily down the Hedge Tunnel. The

smallest fairy had a very fat ladybird clamped under one arm.

"What a boring, grubby little hedge," said the tallest fairy, looking around. She brushed at an imaginary speck of dirt on her pink rose-petal dress.

"I wouldn't have brought you if I wathn't thure the inkcapth were here, Glitter," said Glee earnestly. "Frilly needth lotth of inkcapth for the competithion." She landed on the ground and released her ladybird, which immediately sat down and started panting.

"What competition are they talking about?" Tiptoe whispered.

"The Inter-Pet Competition," said Sesame. She blushed when the others stared at her. "I know it's not very cool or anything, but, well – it's next week."

"Not cool?" Brilliance echoed. "Not cool? It's the saddest fairy competition of the year!"

"Ooh, my beetle's awfully obedient," Kelpie squeaked in a high, breathy voice. "Ooh, my earthworm's ever so much longer than yours."

The fairies giggled. Sesame blushed even deeper. "I like it," she said. "I'm thinking of entering Target this year." The glossy little ant twitched his antennae at the mention of his name.

"For what?" asked Brilliance in amazement.

"For . . . for the ant with the best sense of direction," Sesame muttered.

Brilliance clapped her hand to her forehead. "I'm speechless," she said.

"That'd be a first," Kelpie muttered.

"Shh!" Ping hissed crossly, waving at them. "I'm trying to listen. They're saying something about the spots on their ladybird's back."

". . . everyone knowth that inkcapth give ladybirdth more thpotth," Glee was saying. "If we find thome we can feed

Frilly and she'th bound to win the thpottietht ladybird!"

Brilliance sniggered. Ping bashed her. The Naughty Fairies wriggled and shifted to get a better look at the Ambrosia fairies. Frilly had stopped panting and was now sniffing the ground. She started waddling towards the bramble patch.

Kelpie suddenly stuck out her fist. "Naughty Fairies!" she hissed.

This was their code for mischief.

"Nightmare food!" whispered Tiptoe after a moment, and put her fist on Kelpie's.

"No such thing for you, is there Tiptoe?" Nettle joked. "Nightingale fondue."

"Negative feet," Ping added.

"Natterjack fog!" said Brilliance.

"Gnome, um . . . fossil!"

"Gnome starts with a 'g', Sesame," said Kelpie impatiently. "You're supposed to say something beginning with NF, not GF. Oh, never mind. Fly, fly . . ."

"To the SKY!" the others whispered, and lifted their hands into the air.

"Listen, Frilly's coming this way," Kelpie said. "Let's capture her and make her 'thpotth' disappear completely!"

"You know a spell that does that?" asked Tiptoe, wide-eyed.

Kelpie waved her barbecued berry at Tiptoe. "Who needs spells?"

Frilly stuck her black nose into the Naughty Fairies' bramble patch. She hardly had time to blink before eight fairy hands grabbed her. Kelpie smeared the remains of her barbecued berry on Frilly's back. The ladybird's spots disappeared in a smudge of red berry juice, one by one.

"I rather like the effect," said Brilliance, releasing Frilly, who shot out

13

of the bramble patch as fast as her fat
legs would carry her.

Frilly collapsed at Glee's feet and
panted pathetically. Glee went white.
"Frilly!" she screeched. "Your
THPOTTH!"

The Naughty Fairies stifled their
giggles and watched.

"Your lovely thpotth!" Glee wailed.
"Where did they go?"

Glitter frowned. She bent down and
touched the ladybird's back. Pulling

back in disgust, she stared at her sticky
fingers. "Berry juice!" she hissed.

Kelpie jumped to her feet.

"Oooh!" she shouted. "Poor Fwilly's
thpotth have all gone away!"

"Run!" Brilliance yelled, as the
Ambrosia Academy fairies swung
round.

"You St Juniper's fairies are
pathetic!" Glitter shouted back.

"You're the pathetic ones!" Kelpie
crowed. "Falling for a trick like that!

You're all thad, thtupid and thilly!"

"We'll get you for this!" yelled Gloss, the third Ambrosia fairy.

Laughing, the Naughty Fairies rushed back through the brambles – back to the safety of St Juniper's flowerpot towers.

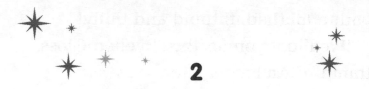

2

The Furriest Bumblebee

"The look on Glee's face!" Ping sighed, as they all collapsed on their foxglove sleeping bags.

"I thought Glee was going to pop," grinned Nettle, putting her ear spiders on her acorn bedside table.

"It was OK," said Brilliance, a little grumpily.

"Just because you didn't think of it, Brilliance," Tiptoe said.

"I do my best," said Kelpie with a smirk. "Anyway, I hate those Ambrosia fairies. They're so smug."

There was a crashing sound outside the window. Looking a little dazed, Flea zoomed in and landed on Kelpie's bed with a loud thud.

"Flea just bumped into the window frame," Sesame guessed, as she put Target the ant on the floor. "I don't think he can see out, Kelpie."

Kelpie stroked her bumblebee. "He's fine," she said, and kissed his furry head.

"Are you sure that's not his bottom?" Sesame asked.

The other fairies giggled. Flea was so furry that it was nearly impossible to tell one end from the other.

"Flea hates haircuts," Kelpie said. She pushed the long black and yellow fur out of the bumblebee's eyes.

"Tie his fur up on top of his head," Nettle suggested.

Kelpie snorted. "He'll look like an idiot."

"That's better than looking like a mop," Brilliance said.

"Hey!" Sesame squeaked, looking up

from examining her damaged wing. "You should enter Flea for the Inter-Pet Competition!"

"As if!" Kelpie said scornfully.

Sesame's eyes were bright. "I'm serious, Kelpie! He'd win the furriest bumblebee category for sure. The prizes are really good. You get a lovely trophy, and Flea gets a year's supply of fur products."

"I'm not entering Flea," Kelpie repeated. "My hedge cred would totally tumble."

"Since when did you care about hedge cred, Kelpie?" Nettle asked.

"I don't care," Kelpie said immediately.

"So you'll enter him?" Sesame pleaded. "It'll be good fun, Kelpie. I'll be there with Target, remember."

"Yeah, us and a bunch of Ambrosia fairies," Kelpie said. "I'd rather poke my eyes out with hedgehog prickles."

"Shame," Sesame sighed. "I'd love it if we could take the trophy off Ambrosia Academy. They win it every year."

"Get over it, Sesame," Kelpie said, after a moment's silence. "I'm not entering Flea, and that's final."

At breakfast the next day, Kelpie was strangely quiet. Flea peered up at her through his shaggy fringe and laid his head on her knee.

"Pass the elderberry juice," Tiptoe said, prodding her.

"Hmm?" Kelpie stared at her. "What?"

"The elderberry juice," Tiptoe repeated. "It's next to you. Are you OK, Kelpie?"

"Why shouldn't I be OK?" Kelpie demanded. "Why is everyone on my back?"

"No one's on your back," Nettle said, after a startled silence.

"Going on and on about the Inter-Pet

Competition last night," Kelpie said in a fierce voice. "Enter Flea, enter Flea, blah blah blah. I said no, didn't I?"

"Too right you did," Brilliance said, taking a sip of elderberry juice. "Entering that competition would be like wearing a sign on your head saying 'kick me, I'm stupid'."

"It's all your fault, Sesame," Kelpie growled, pushing her honeycake round and round her plate.

"I only said—" Sesame began.

"I know what you said," Kelpie said

moodily. "You said I was letting the Ambrosia fairies win that stinking trophy. Well, they're not winning it. Hear that? I'm entering Flea, whether you like it or not."

Brilliance choked on her elderberry juice.

"That's fantastic!" Sesame squealed. "You won't regret it, Kelpie!"

"I'm regretting it already," said Kelpie furiously, pushing back her chair and stalking out of the Dining Flowerpot. Flea buzzed after her.

Outside in the courtyard, Dame Lacewing's pet beetle, Pipsqueak, was sitting patiently underneath the dandelion clock. Dame Lacewing, Deputy Head of St Juniper's and scary Fairy Maths teacher, was backing away from him very slowly.

"Stay," Dame Lacewing commanded, looking down her long nose at Pipsqueak. "Stay."

Pipsqueak honked and trotted up to her in a friendly manner.

"I said stay!" Dame Lacewing roared.

"Entering the Inter-Pet Competition,

Dame Lacewing?" Kelpie asked.

"Yes," Dame Lacewing said shortly, glancing round at Kelpie. "In theory." She looked a bit depressed as she stared at Pipsqueak.

"So am I," Kelpie said gloomily.

Dame Lacewing looked surprised. "I wouldn't have thought the competition was your kind of thing."

"It's not," Kelpie said, even more gloomily. "But I'm entering it anyway."

Dame Lacewing regarded her. "As you never take advice, Kelpie," she said, "I won't give you any. I'll just say that if you're going to do it, do it properly."

She clicked her tongue at Pipsqueak and strode away across the courtyard. Kelpie stared after her.

"Come on, Flea," she said after a moment. "Let's go and ask Turnip if he has any food that will make you extra furry."

*

"I can't believe how seriously you're taking this competition," Brilliance said to Kelpie a few days later. "Extra furry food rations for Flea? Keeping him on a leash all week, to stop him flying through the Hedge and rubbing off his fur? Washing his coat?"

"And combing it," Nettle added.

"It's more than you do to your own hair," Tiptoe said.

"If I'm going to do this, I'm going to do it properly," Kelpie said, looking up from grooming Flea. The bumblebee's coat was looking extremely glossy and fine now that she'd washed and combed it. It hung down almost to his feet, and fell in a neat parting away from his eyes.

"Kelpie's right," said Sesame, stroking Target. The ant purred at her. "Target and I have been practising his sense of direction in the Strawberry Patch all week. The competition's the

day after tomorrow, after all."

"Look at you both!" Brilliance said in disgust. "You've turned into goody-goodies."

Kelpie pointed her hair thistle at Brilliance. "Say that again, and I'll—"

"Shut up, the pair of you," said Ping sharply. "Look Brilliance, Kelpie and Sesame are entering the competition whether you like it or not. So stop sniping at each other, will you?"

Brilliance glowered. "Goody-goodies," she said again. "Ow!"

The hair thistle bounced off Brilliance's head and landed back at Kelpie's feet. Kelpie calmly took up the

thistle again and went back to combing Flea's fur.

"I'm taking Pong to the Meadow for some exercise," said Ping. Pong was Ping's dragonfly. "I want to ride him as much as I can before he starts hibernating. Who's coming?"

"I will," said Kelpie. "Flea's going

mad, cooped up on the end of his leash. He can fly around the Meadow for a bit. He won't spoil his fur doing that."

"I'll bring Target too," said Sesame at once. "The sense of direction course is going to be in the Meadow, so he could use the practice."

"I just want to do a bit of flying," said Nettle.

"The open spaces of the Meadow are great for that," Tiptoe agreed.

"OK," said Brilliance sulkily when the others looked at her. "I'll come."

Kelpie jumped on Flea's back, taking care not to ruffle his fur.

"You should use your own wings for a change," said Brilliance. "If you're so keen on keeping Flea perfect."

"I don't want him to get lost," Kelpie said, kicking Flea gently. "See you there."

The bumblebee flew out of the window. His silky fur streamed out

behind him like a cloak. Kelpie
carefully directed him through the
widest part of the Hedge, and out into
the Meadow on the far side.

The Meadow looked golden in the evening sunlight. Kelpie brought Flea down in a nice wide clearing, and fixed his leash to its longest hole. Flea grumbled and wriggled, and looked hopefully at Kelpie.

"Oh, all right," said Kelpie, relenting. "You can go off the leash for a bit. Just stay in the air, and avoid the grasses, OK?"

Flea buzzed in triumph and kicked up into the sky. Kelpie admired his sleek new shape as he darted and bounced on the breezes that ruffled the Meadow grasses.

"He looks good," Brilliance admitted, landing next to Kelpie. Nettle followed.

"He's a winner for sure," Sesame said confidently, setting Target down.

"Oops," said Tiptoe, almost landing on Target. "Sorry, Sesame."

Ping appeared, looping the loop on Pong's back. Kelpie admired her technique for a bit, then turned and looked for Flea.

But the bumblebee was nowhere to be seen.

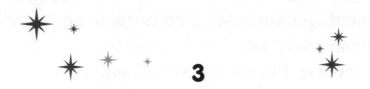

3

Hair Today, Gone Tomorrow

"He'll be back," Kelpie said, staring into the sky.

"You said that two dandelion seeds ago," Sesame said.

The fairies stood together in the clearing and scanned the horizon. The sun was so low that the light skimmed the ground, nearly blinding them.

"Can you see Flea from up there, Ping?" Brilliance called, as the dragonfly swooped overhead.

"Nothing!" Ping called back, pulling Pong.

"He'll be back," Kelpie insisted. "He never goes far."

The other fairies exchanged

significant glances. The sky was completely empty of bumblebees.

"What if he's got lost?" Tiptoe said.

"Don't be stupid," Kelpie snapped. "He's a bee. Bees don't get lost."

"Maybe he's hurt," Nettle suggested, looking anxious.

"Do birds eat bumblebees?" Sesame asked.

Kelpie threw her hands in the air. "Thanks, guys," she said. "Lost. Hurt. Eaten. Anything else?"

"Don't get angry," Brilliance said. "It's not our fault."

"So it's my fault is it?" Kelpie demanded.

"There's no point talking to you when you get like this," said Brilliance, flapping her wings crossly. "Come on, let's split up and look."

Brilliance, Nettle, Tiptoe and Sesame rose into the air together and joined Ping and Pong. Kelpie was left standing alone on the ground.

"Are you coming?" Nettle called down to her.

"I'll wait here," Kelpie muttered. "Flea might come back."

With a pain in her heart, Kelpie watched her friends fly away. She wanted to go with them and look for Flea. But Kelpie had a big problem.

She didn't know how to fly.

It was something she'd never told her friends. Whoever heard of a fairy that couldn't fly? They'd laugh at her.

She flapped her wings cautiously. They creaked and groaned. Her feet didn't want to leave the ground. She turned her face up to the sky.

"Flea!" she called out forlornly. "Come back!"

When the others returned, Kelpie was sitting on the ground with her chin on her knees.

"We had no luck," Brilliance said, landing next to her. "What about you?"

"I flew around a bit," Kelpie lied. "But I couldn't see him."

"He's probably gone back to school," Sesame said. Target stuck his black head out of one of her pockets.

"Yeah, that's probably it," Nettle agreed.

"We should head back," Tiptoe said.

"It's getting dark," said Ping, from somewhere above their heads. "Pong hates the dark."

"I'm going to look a bit longer," said Kelpie. "I'll see you back at school."

"Suit yourself," said Brilliance.

Kelpie watched her friends fly up into the sky and head towards the Hedge.

"Good one, Kelpie," she muttered. "So how are you going to get home?"

With no other choice, Kelpie started walking. The Meadow grasses looked impossibly tall from down here, and cast long black shadows across her path. She called Flea's name hopefully, but there was no answering buzz.

She plodded on. The light was fading rapidly. Kelpie tried not to think about how far it was to the Hedge, or how dark the Hedge would be by the time she reached it. Why oh why had she never learned to fly?

"Stupid, glittery wings," she said savagely. She tried flapping them again, and then ran around and jumped a bit. But when she stumbled over a thick, woody grass stem and bumped her head on the ground, she gave up.

Kelpie never cried. But there was a

suspicious watery feeling around her eyes that wouldn't go away. She rubbed her head and blinked, pushing the watery feeling away.

Something was lying across the path. Kelpie leaned down and picked it up, turning it over in her hand.

It was a pale pink rose petal.

We'll get you for this! Gloss's voice floated across Kelpie's memory. She gasped.

The Ambrosia Academy fairies had kidnapped Flea!

Brilliance kicked Kelpie's bed. "Get up, lazy! We'll be late for breakfast!"

Kelpie opened her bleary eyes. "Don't want breakfast," she mumbled, and turned over.

"What time did you get in?" Tiptoe asked, pulling on her spider-silk cardigan.

Kelpie had crept into bed just

moments before dawn.

"Late," she croaked.

"Any sign of Flea?" Nettle asked.

Kelpie sat up. Her hair stuck out sideways. "He's been kidnapped, OK?" she snapped.

The others gasped, and clustered even closer around Kelpie's bed.

"Kidnapped?"

"Why?"

"How do you know?"

"I found a rose petal," Kelpie said. "Pink, just like the ones the Ambrosia fairies wear."

"It's because of that joke you played on Frilly!" Brilliance guessed. "How are you going to get Flea back?"

Kelpie's head hurt from where she'd bumped it on the grass stem.

"Why don't you all just go away?" she growled.

"I'll get you some honeycakes for Fairy Science," Tiptoe promised, backing out of the room.

"GO AWAY!" Kelpie roared.

The next thing Kelpie knew, the school bluebells were ringing for the start of lessons. She crawled out of bed and stuck her head in the walnut-shell washbasin full of rainwater which stood

by the dormitory door. Then she walked downstairs and across the courtyard to the Science Flowerpot, stifling a yawn with the back of her hand. Her temper glowed fiercely as she thought of the Ambrosia fairies. Was Flea OK? How was she going to get him back?

"Good of you to join us, Kelpie," Dame Taffeta said as Kelpie walked sulkily into the flowerpot.

"Yada yada yada," Kelpie muttered, and threw herself down in a seat next to Brilliance.

Dame Taffeta's ears turned a very faint pink. "See me after the lesson," she said.

"Whatever." Kelpie laid her head on her desk.

"She's lost her bumblebee, Dame Taffeta," Sesame explained.

"That's no excuse for rudeness," said Dame Taffeta, pursing her lips. "Today, we are making love potions."

Groans spread through the class.

"Love potions," Dame Taffeta repeated loudly, "are full of delicate ingredients. Please do not mash them, bash them or cut them in any way. A good love potion simply simmers. It must not be disturbed until the optimum point, or it is liable to explode."

Kelpie gave a snore. Brilliance elbowed her. "Wake up," she hissed. "Do you want a detention?"

"I just want to be left alone," Kelpie mumbled.

"I'll make your love potion for you, Kelpie," Tiptoe whispered, passing a honeycake surreptitiously across the desk. Kelpie turned her head away. Honeycakes reminded her of Flea.

Soon, the Science Flowerpot was full of delicious simmering smells. Several fairies were looking a bit glazed. One fairy was staring entranced at her reflection in a dewdrop that was sitting on the window sill.

"You can never be too careful with love potions," said Dame Taffeta, striding up and down the flowerpot with a handful of small green leaves. "You should always have a sprig of bitter cress on hand, to counteract the effects."

"I think Kelpie needs a bit of love potion herself," Nettle said, as Kelpie bashed at a stem of lovage with a hard, angry look on her face.

Kelpie flung down the lovage. "Why can't you all just leave me ALONE?" she shouted.

Dame Taffeta came bustling over. "I won't have this behaviour in my class, Kelpie," she began.

"Fine," said Kelpie. "I'll leave." And she pushed over a nearby acorn cup.

A purple blaze shot into the air as the potion hit the floor and exploded. Dame

Taffeta shrieked and clutched her head.

"Dame Taffeta's hair!" gasped
Brilliance in horror. "It's gone!"

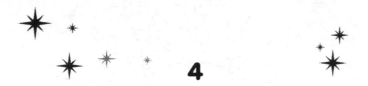

4

Ambrosia Academy

Dame Taffeta ran out of the flowerpot. There was a deathly silence. Several fairies stared in horror at their simmering potions, and backed away from them extremely carefully.

"Don't look at me like that!" Kelpie protested, as her friends gazed at her with round eyes. "How was I supposed to know it would explode?"

"Dame Taffeta said it would!" Brilliance hissed, stepping cautiously over the burned patch on the ground. "Don't you ever listen, Kelpie?"

"I thought Dame Taffeta looked all right," said Ping.

"But she's bald!" Tiptoe wailed.

"Apart from being bald," Ping added.

"Poor Dame Taffeta!" Sesame said.
She felt her long silky ponytail and
tucked it inside her dress.

The fairies all started murmuring and
whispering. No one knew what to do.
In a strange way, everyone felt quite
relieved when Dame Lacewing
marched into the flowerpot. Several
fairies started asking questions.

"Is Dame Taffeta all right, Dame
Lacewing?"

"Will her hair grow again?"

"Is the rest of the lesson cancelled?"

asked a hopeful fairy at the back.

"Dame Taffeta most certainly is not all right," Dame Lacewing said. "Would you be all right if a fairy had thrown a dangerous potion at you?"

"I didn't know it would explode, Dame Lacewing," Kelpie began.

"Enough, Kelpie," Dame Lacewing snapped. "I am disgusted by your behaviour. Dame Fuddle and I are meeting later today to discuss your future at St Juniper's."

Kelpie felt a strange weakness around her knees.

"You will all do this worksheet for the rest of the lesson." Dame Lacewing walked up and down the flowerpot, distributing petal papers which the fairies all took quietly. "I don't want to hear another word until the bluebell rings. Is that understood?"

Kelpie stared at her worksheet with blurred eyes. None of it made sense.

Your future at St Juniper's – your future
. . . Dame Lacewing's words whispered
through her head like a horrible
creeping mist.

"She won't expel you," Brilliance
whispered.

"How do you know?" Kelpie
muttered, pushing the worksheet away.

"I don't," Brilliance admitted.

"Be QUIET at the back!" Dame
Lacewing roared.

Silence fell once more.

It was the most horrible day Kelpie
could remember. Everywhere she went,
fairies stared at her. There were terrible
rumours that Dame Taffeta's hair would
never grow back, and it was all Kelpie's
fault. Apart from her friends, no one
else talked to Kelpie all day.

"I saw Dame Lacewing going into
Dame Fuddle's study just now," said
Sesame in a low voice, as the Naughty
Fairies clustered together gloomily in

the courtyard after the final lesson of the day. "They'll probably send for you soon, Kelpie."

"Well, I'm not sticking around long enough for that," Kelpie said, holding her head high. "I'm going to look for Flea. If they want me, they can wait until I come back."

Her friends gasped.

"You can't!" Tiptoe squeaked. "You'll just make things worse!"

"How can things be worse?" Kelpie asked. "I'm going to be expelled! Well, they aren't expelling me until I find Flea."

"Do you want us to come too?" Brilliance asked. "We could all fly to the Meadow together."

Kelpie's eyes got that suspicious watery feeling again.

"Are you crying, Kelpie?" Sesame asked.

"Of course not," Kelpie snapped. If

her friends came, she'd have to tell them that she couldn't fly. On top of everything that had happened today, she couldn't face it. "I'm going to do this by myself. Thanks and everything, but I'm the one in trouble. There's no point you getting in trouble too."

Kelpie could hear Turnip clattering his pans as she crept around the back of the Kitchen Flowerpot, to where Caddy the school grasshopper was tethered. Her pockets were bulging with honeycakes. The grasshopper sniffed at her pockets with interest as she untied him.

"Good boy," Kelpie whispered, climbing on his back. She glanced at the kitchen door. If Turnip saw her . . .

"Time to go to the Wood." She tapped the grasshopper's sides with her feet, and Caddy jumped away towards the Hedge.

Kelpie wasn't sure what she was
going to do when she got to Ambrosia
Academy. As Caddy hopped through
the tall grasses of the Meadow, she
clung on and tried to make a plan.
She'd never been to Ambrosia Academy
before. It wasn't somewhere that St
Juniper's fairies ever chose to visit.

Caddy hopped on until the Meadow thinned and Kelpie could see the edges of the Wood. Brown leaves lay on the ground, and there was a smell of mushrooms and mice. When the turrets of Ambrosia Academy came into view, Kelpie reined in Caddy and slipped off his back. She gave him a honeycake.

"If I'm not back in half a dandelion, go back to school," she said, patting him on the back. Then, wriggling over twigs and sliding down damp leaves, Kelpie made her way towards Ambrosia Academy.

It was already early evening, and the sky had darkened. Fairy lights flickered on all sides, and there was a smell of roasting chestnuts in the air. With wide eyes, Kelpie stared up at Ambrosia Academy's magnificent toadstool turrets. They were grand beyond imagination.

She threw herself into the shadow of a

toadstool stem as a group of Ambrosia
fairies walked past.

". . . fairy cakes are the easiest things
in the world," drawled a familiar voice.
"Back at home, our cook practically
makes them behind her back."

"I do think Lady Mallow could have
shown us something a bit more
special," said another bored-sounding

voice. "Honestly, who ever makes fairy cakes these days?"

"I think they're delithious," squeaked the third voice. "Though they do terrible thingth to my waitht."

A very fat ladybird trotted past the toadstool stem. It suddenly stopped, and stared straight at Kelpie. Kelpie stared back. Suddenly, she wished she'd never covered Frilly in berry juice. Ladybirds had very long memories.

Frilly growled.

"What'th the matter, poochkinth?" asked Glee, bending down to stroke her ladybird's neck. Frilly growled again. In awful slow motion, the three Ambrosia fairies turned their heads.

"Well, well, well," said Glitter in a satisfied-sounding voice. "The rat's in the trap."

Gloss laughed as Kelpie stepped out of the shadows.

"A rat in the motht horrible outfit I've ever theen," said Glee, staring at Kelpie's bumblewool jumper dress with horror.

"I'm not the rat around here," Kelpie snarled. "Where's my bumblebee?"

Glitter's eyes flickered. "What bumblebee?"

Kelpie was hanging on to her temper by a thread. "I want Flea back," she said. She raised her fists very slightly.

Glitter paused. "Oh, that bumblebee," she said after a moment. "You're welcome to him. He's been nothing but trouble since he, er – flew in here. He's in a pen behind you."

Kelpie looked over her shoulder. She walked towards a neat twig pen half hidden in the shadows. "Flea?" she whispered through the darkness. There was an ecstatic buzzing sound. "Are you OK?"

A small, bald and very cold-looking

insect stood in the middle of the pen. It blinked sadly at her.

"Flea?" Kelpie choked. "Is that you?"

The Ambrosia fairies burst out laughing. Blind with fury, Kelpie spun round and jumped on Glitter.

"Thtop her, Gloth!" Glee screeched.

"She's bigger than me," Gloss said uneasily.

Kelpie and Glitter rolled over on the wet ground. Glitter screeched and wriggled, but Kelpie held her firmly. With one free hand, Kelpie scooped up a blob of mud and dangled it over Glitter's face.

"Not the mud!" Glitter wept. "Not the mud!"

"You stinking piece of fungus," Kelpie hissed. "You shaved Flea's coat off."

"I didn't!" Glitter squeaked. "He just turned up like that!"

"Liar!" Kelpie roared, and smeared the mud through Glitter's hair.

Glitter howled. Tugging the bedraggled pink fairy to her feet, Kelpie tore off Glitter's fluffy cardigan and backed away to Flea's pen. Flea was buzzing furiously, trying to pull his tether out of the ground.

"How could you shave a bumblebee in the autumn?" Kelpie shouted. "How's he supposed to stay warm?" She shook the cardigan at Glitter, who was now shivering. "See how you like

it!" She untied Flea and wrapped the cardigan tenderly around his bald shoulders. Flea snuggled gratefully into its woolly warmth, and nudged at the honeycakes in Kelpie's pocket.

As Kelpie rose into the air on Flea's cardiganed back, she shook her fist at the Ambrosia fairies below. "I'll get revenge if it's the last thing I do," she said, giving them her most terrible glare. And Flea shot away, through the trees and out into the wide, dark Meadow.

5

Kelpie's Luck

Kelpie and Flea zoomed back to St Juniper's in record time. Without his coat, Flea flew like an arrow. At least that was something, Kelpie thought bitterly.

She brought Flea down into the darkened courtyard of St Juniper's and through the dormitory window. After adjusting Flea's cardigan, Kelpie straightened up and glared at her friends. "The first fairy to make a stupid comment will get their heads dunked in the washbasin," she hissed.

There was an appalled silence as the Naughty Fairies stared at Flea.

"It suits him," said Sesame weakly.

"Don't be stupid," said Brilliance. "He looks like a flying ant."

Ping stepped in and caught Kelpie's flailing fists. "Brilliance meant to say, that's a good thing," she said, giving Brilliance a warning glance.

"First Dame Taffeta, now Flea," Nettle said. "There's a lot of baldness about today."

"How did he get like that?" Tiptoe whispered.

"The Ambrosia fairies shaved him,"

Kelpie said. "I'll get them back for this."

"You probably won't get the chance," Brilliance said. "Dame Lacewing's been looking everywhere for you."

With an awful lurch, Kelpie remembered. "Do you know what they've decided?" she whispered.

Her friends shook their heads.

"But the good news is, Dame Taffeta's grown her hair back," Nettle added.

"I have to go and see Dame Lacewing," said Kelpie heavily. "I can't put it off any longer. Come on, Flea. You'd better come too."

Kelpie ignored the sideways glances as she marched across the dark courtyard and over to Dame Lacewing's study. Flea buzzed overhead, the spider-silk ribbons of his cardigan flapping in the wind.

Dame Lacewing opened the door on

Kelpie's first tentative knock. "The wanderer returns," she said. "You'd better come in, Kelpie."

Trying to stop her knees from shaking, Kelpie stepped into Dame Lacewing's study. She stared at the pressed flower pictures and the flickering twig fire in the centre of the flowerpot. Pipsqueak was lying beside the fire, his tummy pointing at the flames.

"Sit down," Dame Lacewing said.

Flea buzzed through the door as Dame Lacewing went to shut it.

"I brought Flea," Kelpie said stiffly, still standing up. "I didn't want to leave him alone."

"What on earth happened to him?" Dame Lacewing exclaimed, staring at Flea.

"Are you going to expel me?" Kelpie asked.

Dame Lacewing fingered the ribbons

on Flea's cardigan. "Are you going to tell me what happened here?"

Kelpie shrugged. "Nothing to tell," she said. "So, are you going to expel me?"

"Kelpie," said Dame Lacewing, "I have been at St Juniper's for many years, and I can usually tell when there's something to tell. If you know what I mean."

Kelpie stared at her fingers. Then, without really meaning to, she told Dame Lacewing what had happened. Dame Lacewing listened carefully.

"That's quite a story," said Dame Lacewing when Kelpie had finished. "It has no bearing on our decision, however."

Kelpie hung her head.

"Dame Taffeta has successfully regrown her hair," Dame Lacewing continued. "She's so pleased with the results that she doesn't want us to expel you." She gave a slight smile. "The situation with your bumblebee doesn't excuse your behaviour in the Science Flowerpot, but it does explain it. You are one of the naughtiest fairies in the school, Kelpie," she added, "but I don't think that you are malicious. We have decided to limit your punishment to two weeks' detention."

Kelpie swallowed. "Thank you, Dame Lacewing," she whispered.

Dame Lacewing pulled open the door. "Now, go and apologise to Dame Taffeta," she said. "And if you ask her nicely, she might give you some hair-growing potion for Flea."

Dame Taffeta beamed when she opened the door. "Kelpie dear," she said fondly. "Come in."

Unlike Dame Lacewing's tidy study, Dame Taffeta's room was strewn with papers, pots, cups and scarves draped over every surface. A smell of lavender oil and damp socks filled the air.

"I'm sorry about what happened in Fairy Science, Dame Taffeta," Kelpie said, a little nervously.

"Of course you are," Dame Taffeta said. She patted her new golden curls, which were piled neatly on top of her head. "You didn't do it on purpose, after all."

"Well, I did," Kelpie began. "I just didn't realise . . ."

Dame Taffeta laughed and waved her hand. "Let's not dwell on the past. Tell me, do you like my new hair?"

"It's very nice," said Kelpie truthfully. Dame Taffeta's new hair was certainly very shiny, and so golden that it almost hurt to look at it.

"Really, I feel a hundred years younger," Dame Taffeta sighed. "And if it hadn't been for you, I would never have worked out the potion formula."

"I'm, um, pleased for you," said
Kelpie. She was getting a headache. It
was hard being nice to teachers.

"Gracious me, whatever happened to
your bumblebee?" Dame Taffeta asked,
noticing Flea for the first time.

"It's a long story, Dame Taffeta," said
Kelpie. "And, um, I wondered if I could
ask you a favour?"

Dame Taffeta was staring at her
reflection in the long tin-foil mirror on
the wall. "Anything you like, dear," she
said generously, turning to the side a

little to admire the back of her head.

"Do you have any of your hair-growing potion left?" Kelpie asked in a rush. "You see, I thought perhaps we could use it on Flea. He had a little . . . accident, and the air's really cold at the moment, and . . ."

Dame Taffeta waved her hand at the lavender- and sock-smelling acorn cup standing on her desk. "Help yourself," she said. "If dear Flea feels half as good as I do with some new hair, how can I refuse?"

Kelpie picked up the acorn cup. There was a dark purple liquid swilling around in the bottom.

"Smear it on to his skin and leave it for one dandelion," Dame Taffeta suggested. "Flea's hair will come back as good as new." She gave a girlish giggle and patted her curls again. "Or perhaps, even better?"

Kelpie carefully carried the potion

back across the courtyard. Not only was she not being expelled, she'd got some stuff to grow Flea's fur back in record time! She'd never had so much luck in one go.

Her friends clustered around her as she came into the dormitory.

"Was Dame Lacewing totally furious?"

"Have you been expelled?"

"Why does that cup smell of socks?"

Kelpie set the acorn cup down very carefully. "No, no, and I don't know," she said. "But I do know that if we put this stuff on Flea, his fur will grow back in time for the Inter-Pet Competition. So who's going to help me put it on?"

The atmosphere in the Naughty Fairies' dormitory was brighter than it had been for days. Chattering and laughing, they smeared gloops of purple hair-growing potion all over Flea. They wrapped him up neatly in a

leaf, so he looked like a small green parcel.

Then they went to bed, ready for the Inter-Pet Competition the following day.

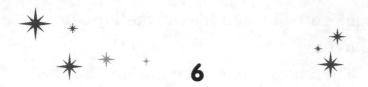

6

Fly, Fly, to the SKY!

In Kelpie's dream, she kicked Frilly's
bottom so hard that the fat little
ladybird scooted across the floor like a
small spotted football. It was one of the
best dreams she'd ever had.

Opening her eyes, she stared at the
ceiling. It was the day of the
competition. The day that she got her
revenge on the Ambrosia fairies by
winning the furriest bumblebee trophy.
She pictured herself holding the trophy
high in the air, then dropping it on
Glitter's foot.

Sesame screamed.

"What?" Kelpie sat bolt upright.

Sesame pointed at Flea with a

shaking hand. "Look!"

The leaf had fallen off, and now lay in tatters around Flea's feet.

"Is he supposed to be that colour?" asked Nettle, after a moment.

Flea blinked at them from beneath a luminous fringe.

Finding her voice at last, Kelpie yelped in horror. "He's PINK!"

"And green," Brilliance added.

"And yellow," said Tiptoe. "On his tummy, look."

"He's purple behind the ears too," Ping said. "Twinkle-tastic."

Flea buzzed at them and tossed his head. His pink, green, yellow and purple fur shook and shimmered.

"Well, at least it grew back," Sesame offered.

"It's not as long as before," Nettle pointed out. "You can see his knees, look."

"I can't enter him looking like this!" Kelpie shouted. "Everyone will laugh at him!"

"Everyone was going to laugh at him anyway," said Brilliance. "I mean, it is the Inter-Pet Competition."

"Shut up, Brilliance," Kelpie snarled. "I'm going to see Dame Taffeta!"

Kelpie pushed open the Dining Flowerpot doors with a crash. Fairies and staff looked up from their clover buns and stared as Kelpie marched up

to the staff table, followed more
cautiously by her friends.

Kelpie crashed her fist on the table in
front of the startled Dame Taffeta. "Why
did you do it?" she demanded. "Revenge?"

"Kelpie," Dame Lacewing thundered, before anyone else could speak. "How dare you talk to a member of staff this way? Did our conversation yesterday teach you nothing?"

"Do what, Kelpie dear?" Dame Taffeta asked, looking bewildered.

"Turn my bumblebee into a joke!" Kelpie roared. "Look at him!"

Dame Taffeta, along with the rest of the St Juniper's staff and pupils, looked up as Flea soared into the Dining Flowerpot in all his rainbow glory. There were gasps and whistles. Several fairies laughed.

Dame Taffeta looked pale. "How long did you leave the potion on?" she asked.

Kelpie paused. A faint memory was nagging at her. "Overnight," she said.

"Overnight?" Dame Taffeta gasped. "I said, just one dandelion! No wonder he's such an assortment of colours!"

Flea did a multicoloured loop-the-loop, zooming down to snatch a honeycake from Dame Honey's plate.

"Just . . . just one dandelion?" Kelpie repeated. She suddenly felt rather hot around her ears.

"Whoops," said Tiptoe.

"You never listen, Kelpie," Brilliance muttered.

Dame Lacewing stood up. "I think," she said in a dangerous voice, "that

84

once again, you owe Dame Taffeta an apology, Kelpie. Don't you agree?"

After lessons, the Naughty Fairies gathered together at the Butterfly Stables. The Inter-Pet Competition was being held in the Meadow in just one dandelion's time.

"Never mind, Kelpie," said Sesame comfortingly, polishing Target's glossy black coat with beeswax. "You already had two weeks of detentions. What's one more week?"

"I can't believe how stupid I was," Kelpie said gloomily, stroking Flea's rainbow fur. "Now the Ambrosia fairies will win the trophy and it's all my fault."

"At least the colour effect will wear off by tomorrow morning," said Nettle. "Flea will be back to his normal black and yellow self then."

"There," said Sesame, straightening

up and patting Target on the head. "He couldn't gleam more if he was a firefly."

"He looks great, Sesame," said Tiptoe.

"I know," Sesame agreed. "His sense of direction is still rubbish, so he probably won't win. But at least he'll be the smartest ant in the showring."

Nettle looked at the nearby dandelion

clock. "We'd better go if we're going to get good seats." Brilliance started to say something, but Nettle held up her hand. "We're all going," she said warningly. "Naughty Fairies do everything together, right?"

"Even nerdy competitions," Ping agreed. "Let's go."

Brilliance, Nettle, Tiptoe and Ping stood up and stretched their wings. Sesame rubbed a bit of fluff off Target's shiny head, then scooped him up and tucked him under her arm.

"You coming, Kelpie?" Nettle asked.

"No," said Kelpie in a low voice. "I can't take Flea looking like this."

"Leave him here then," said Brilliance.

"I can't," said Kelpie, in an even lower voice. "If Flea doesn't come, I can't come either."

"Why not?" Sesame asked. "Just use your own wings for once."

"I can't come," Kelpie muttered, "because – because – I can't fly."

Her friends looked confused.

"Can't fly?" Brilliance repeated. "But . . . but you're a fairy!"

"You think I don't know that?" Kelpie said, glaring at her.

"I don't understand," said Nettle. "Are you saying that your wings don't work?"

"Well, they don't work for me, anyway," Kelpie muttered. Her cheeks felt hot. "I don't want to talk about it, OK? Go to the competition and I'll see you later."

Ping stepped around Kelpie's back and stretched out one of her wings.

"Get off!" Kelpie said angrily, and pulled away from Ping's hands.

There was an odd noise, as if something had just popped into place. Kelpie felt a strange shiver run down her neck.

"No wonder you couldn't fly," Ping murmured. "One of your wings was totally jammed up. Don't you ever stretch them?"

Kelpie was feeling very odd. "Why

would I stretch them?" she snapped.
"They're stupid, useless things. I hardly
ever think about them."

"But Kelpie," said Tiptoe, "didn't
anyone ever tell you that if you don't
use your wings, they just freeze up?"

Ping seized Kelpie's other wing and
stretched it out. There was another
popping noise. Kelpie's stomach
suddenly felt as if it was full of air.

"Try them now," Ping suggested.

"I'll just fall flat on my face and you'll laugh at me," Kelpie whispered.

"Go on, give them a try," Sesame said.

"Just a little flap," Tiptoe added.

"Shut up and go away!" Kelpie roared. She'd never felt so scared in all her life.

Brilliance put her head on one side and folded her arms. "I dare you," she said.

Kelpie's knees felt like water. "A . . . dare?"

"Yup," said Brilliance. "Scared?"

"It's a total waste of time . . ." Kelpie began.

"Dare," Brilliance chanted. "Dare, dare, dare!"

There was nothing for it. Kelpie shut her eyes. She flapped her wings. "There," she said, opening them again. "Told you it was a waste of . . ."

Her voice trailed
away as she
realised she was
hovering off the
ground.

"You're doing
it!" Sesame
shouted.

"Go, Kelpie!"
Nettle
screamed.

"I'm . . . I'm
flying?" Kelpie
whispered.
She felt dizzy.

"Course you're
flying," said
Brilliance. "I dared
you, and you
always do dares. I'm
so brilliant
sometimes, I could
kiss myself."

"I'm the one who stretched her wings," Ping protested.

"I would have done that too, if I'd been closer," Brilliance said airily.

"I'm FLYING!" Kelpie shouted. She flapped her wings again and shot into the sky. "I'm REALLY TRULY FLYING!"

Nettle grinned up at her. "So, are you coming to the competition?"

Kelpie pirouetted in the air, then

came down again to land firmly on Flea's multicoloured back. "You bet," she said. "Who cares if they laugh? I've got a trophy to win!"

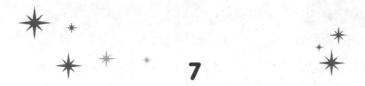

7

A Surprising Trophy

"I don't think I can cheer any more," Nettle said hoarsely, flopping down on her bed.

Kelpie put her trophy reverently on the window sill, where it gleamed in the late evening sunshine.

"It's a great trophy," Brilliance said. "For an—"

"Inter-Pet Competition trophy, I know," said Kelpie. "Don't overdo the praise, will you, Brilliance?"

Sesame looked sadly at Kelpie's trophy.

"Don't look so down, Sesame," said Nettle, putting her arm around Sesame's shoulders. "Target was never

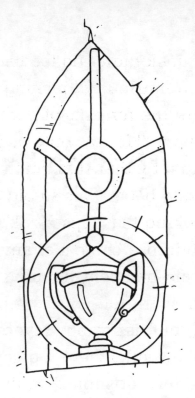

going to win the Ant with the Best
Sense of Direction. You said so
yourself."

"I know," Sesame sighed. "But I
didn't think that his sense of direction
was so bad that he'd end up getting lost
and disappearing completely."

"He'll like the Meadow," Tiptoe
assured her. "There'll be lots of other
ants for him to get lost with."

"Pipsqueak didn't do too badly, did he?" Ping murmured, picking at her teeth with the remains of her raspberry pip lollipop. "He was only beaten at the last minute by that stag beetle."

"The stag beetle was so big and scary-looking that Pipsqueak probably lost on purpose," said Kelpie. She reached for her trophy again and polished its tin-foil glitter with her sleeve. Flea buzzed proudly and rested his chin on her lap.

"Wasn't it funny about Frilly?" Brilliance giggled.

"Serves Glee right for feeding her so many inkcap mushrooms," Sesame said. "She was black all over."

"I could have kissed the judge," Ping agreed.

Kelpie imitated the judge's voice. "'This is the spottiest ladybird section, my dear. The most obedient beetle section is over there.'"

"Shame the Ambrosias won the furriest bumblebee in the end," Nettle sighed.

"Their excuse for a bee would never have beaten Flea in his prime," said Kelpie scornfully, setting her trophy back on the window sill again. "Anyway, this Bees' Knees trophy is bigger and much better. And Glitter was furious."

"Who'd have thought that Flea's knees were so fantastic underneath all that fur?" Ping said.

"I had so many enquiries about Flea's rainbow fur that I'm thinking of going into business with Dame Taffeta's hair-growing potion," said Kelpie thoughtfully. "We could have a whole Meadow full of multicoloured insects."

Brilliance stood up and flexed her wings. "Who's coming for an evening fly, then?" she asked. "The sky's gorgeous out there."

"Me!"

"Count me in!"

Kelpie stretched her wings. "Me too," she said with a grin. "Oh, me most definitely too!"

Caterpillar Thriller

The Naughty Fairies have great plans
to turn Dame Taffeta into a human
catapult, and to beat Ambrosia
Academy in the Butterfly Cup.

But nothing goes quite right.

They'll have to break every rule to
win the fabulous Cup prize!

Sweet Cheat

The May Day Feast is coming . . .
  And that means Turnip the kitchen
pixie's TOFFEE!
  But what's his special ingredient?
  When greedy Tiptoe eats all his
toffee, she needs to find out – fast!

Also available from
Hodder Children's Books

Spells and Smells

Ping has played the biggest practical joke EVER!

But has she gone just too far this time? And now the Tooth Fairy is missing!

Can Ping get herself out of serious trouble by bringing her back?